AMELIARANNE
AND THE
JUMBLE SALE

TOLD·BY
EILEEN·
OSBORNE

PICTURED
BY~S.B.
PEARSE

CO·
PICTURE LIONS

School was over for the day, and most of the boys and girls had set off for home.

But Ameliaranne Stiggins stood looking at the notice board in the passage. On it was pinned a poster, beautifully painted by her teacher, Miss Helen Loveday, which said:

GRAND JUMBLE SALE
in aid of RED CROSS
to be held in
SLEEPY FURROW VILLAGE HALL
on Saturday Afternoon
Please bring everything to
the Hall by Friday evening

Ameliaranne was just admiring all the little drawings in the border when Miss Loveday came out of the classroom.

"Would you like to help me at the Jumble Sale tomorrow, Ameliaranne?" she asked. "We have a lot of things already, and I shall be very glad of a helper on my stall."

"Oh, Miss Helen, I'd love to!" exclaimed Ameliaranne. "But I shall have to ask Mother first, because I usually help her with the little ones on Saturdays."

With that, Ameliaranne lost no time in getting home. In fact, she ran all the way, so that when she burst into the kitchen she only had enough breath left to gasp, "Oh, Mother! Miss Helen has asked me to help her on her stall tomorrow. I *would* like to, but I said I help you with the babies on Saturdays."

"Bless the child!" said Mrs Stiggins, quite taken aback. "You talk so fast I can't make head or tail of it!"

Mrs Stiggins sat down heavily in her favourite chair, and Ameliaranne said it all over again, much slower.

When she had come to the end, Mrs Stiggins thought for a moment, and then she said, "Well, Ameliaranne, I don't see why you shouldn't go. We can soon do the house in the morning, and then I could send the children up to play in Farmer Wheatsheaf's field. He says he's always pleased to have them. And that means I could go to the Sale myself."

Ameliaranne's faced beamed with pleasure as she sat down to her tea.

She was just spreading honey on Wee William's bread when Mrs Stiggins set her cup down and said,

"I've been thinking, Ameliaranne. After tea you could take the things I've put together up to the Hall. They're sure to be busy up there, and you can help Miss Loveday with the ticketing."

So directly after tea Ameliaranne popped on her hat again.

She took the bundle of clothes Mrs Stiggins had put together in one hand, and a box of rock cakes for the Food Stall in the other, and set off up the road.

As soon as Ameliaranne came to the Village Green she saw a crowd of boys and girls, all making for the Hall, and each carrying a basket or a bundle.

There were the Jollyface twins, struggling with one of their father's prize marrows, and Betty Button, whose mother was a dressmaker and could make all sorts of pretty things out of bits and pieces.

And then there was Teddy Carter, who had done his parcel up himself. He was very proud of the slip-knots, which he had learnt at the Cubs.

When Ameliaranne stepped into the Village
Hall it seemed so full of people and clothes she
hardly knew what to do. But Miss Loveday
saw her and called, "Come and help me to sort
the things out."

Ameliaranne first set down her bundle. She
gave the rock cakes to Miss Munday at the Food
Stall, then knelt down beside Miss Loveday and
began to sort the big pile of clothes.

First of all she found all the loose socks,
rolled them up in pairs as her Mother did after
washing day. Then she found a cushion, a scarf
and a coloured ball and placed them between
a pile of books and an old straw hat.

Then she came to a sailor suit that Tommy
Tucker used to wear, and last of all she found
a pair of blue slippers which she gazed at for
a long time. They were the prettiest slippers
she had ever seen. Each of them was made to
look like a rabbit with two fluffy white ears.
There were beads for eyes, and the nose, the
mouth and even the whiskers were in white silk.

"Oh, Miss Helen!" exclaimed Ameliaranne.
"Do look at these pretty shoes! I'm sure they'd
fit our Wee William. How he'd love them!"

"Perhaps your Mother will buy them for
him, dear," said Miss Helen, as she fixed on the
ticket which said 10p.

Then Ameliaranne and Miss Loveday took all the things they had piled on the floor and arranged them on the stall.

They hung a baby's silk dress and some pretty mats on a line at the back. Then came a vase of flowers, the cushion, and a work-box. And in front was the sailor suit.

In the very first row were all the boots and shoes, with the biggest football boots on the outside and Ameliaranne's blue rabbity slippers in the middle.

Then Ameliaranne and Miss Loveday stood
back and looked at their work.

Ameliaranne's face shone with pride as she
exclaimed,

"I think our stall is the nicest of all, don't you,
Miss Helen?"

Miss Helen could not help feeling a little
proud herself.

"Well, I'm sure it's quite *as nice as* any of the
others, Ameliaranne," she smiled.

When Ameliaranne got home she lost no time
in telling her Mother about all the things she
had seen.

And the very last of all she described the
blue rabbity slippers, and begged her Mother
to buy them for Wee William.

But Mrs Stiggins looked doubtful.

"Ten pence is a lot to spend on Wee
William," she said. "And they'd soon be too
small for him."

"Still," she added, as she saw that
Ameliaranne looked quite sad, "we'll see,
when I get to the Hall tomorrow."

The next day Ameliaranne put on her best dress and was at the Village Hall in good time. Everybody was adding last minute touches to their stalls and soon all was in apple-pie order.

On the stroke of two, Ameliaranne and Miss Loveday and all the other helpers stood ready behind their stalls. The door was opened, and the people began to flock in.

Ameliaranne noticed that a lot of the mothers made straight for their stall, and soon she was busy serving people and giving change.

Socks and boots, hats and bonnets, jumpers and skirts disappeared – but no one bought the rabbity slippers.

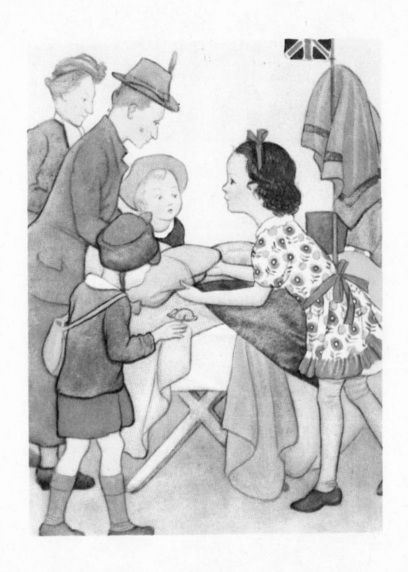

At three o'clock there was a commotion at the door. Ameliaranne saw Teddy Carter's mother run in, looking upset. Her hair was blown by the wind, and she still had her apron on.

"Oh, dear," she panted. "Something dreadful has happened! My little Teddy packed my old black skirt in with the Jumble things, and it has got all my savings in the pocket!"

"Oh, please, Mrs Carter," cried Ameliaranne. "I think I know who bought it! Don't worry, I'll soon get it back for you."

For Ameliaranne had suddenly remembered she had seen Mrs Jollyface going out of the door with a back skirt over her arm.

While everyone stood looking at her in astonishment, Ameliaranne ran out of the Hall and down the road as fast as her legs could carry her.

Mrs Jollyface's house was right at the other end of the village, and by the time Ameliaranne had reached the garden gate, she was quite out of breath and had a stitch in her side. Mrs Jollyface's door was ajar, and, after knocking, Ameliaranne pushed it open and stepped into the kitchen.

There she saw Mrs Jollyface and the twins standing quite still, staring at one another.

Mrs Jollyface had an iron in one hand, and several pound notes in the other. And the Jollyface twins were gazing first at the iron and then at the notes and then back again.

"Well, I never!" gasped Mrs Jollyface at last. "Just look at this, Ameliaranne! Here's a lot of money in the skirt I bought at the Jumble Sale. When I came to iron over the pocket I heard it crackling!"

"Oh, Mrs Jollyface!" Ameliaranne burst out. "I've come to find that money. It's Mrs Carter's, and she's worried because Teddy put the skirt in her bundle by mistake. She keeps all her savings in it."

"Why, the poor soul!" Mrs Jollyface exclaimed. "What a state she must be in! Here, Ameliaranne, take the skirt and all back to her. And look, I'll put the money safe in an envelope, so that you won't drop it."

Ameliaranne picked up the skirt and clutched the envelope tightly in her other hand.

"Please can we come with you, Ameliaranne?" cried the Jollyface twins, who had now recovered from their surprise.

So Ameliaranne set off for the Hall with a Jollyface twin on each side of her.

The twins were smaller than Ameliaranne, so that although they ran as fast as they could, Ameliaranne only had to trot. But she could still feel that nasty stitch in her side, and so she didn't think she could have run back to the Hall as fast as she had come to Mrs Jollyface's, anyway.

At the Village Hall they found Mrs Carter anxiously waiting.

When she saw them, Mrs Carter threw up her hands in joy.

"Ameliaranne," she declared, "you are a fair marvel."

Then she turned to Mrs Stiggins, and said, "There's that child brought back all my savings, safe and sound, almost before we could turn around!"

Mrs Stiggins beamed at Ameliaranne.

"Yes, our Ameliaranne is a good girl," she remarked. "When things go wrong she can generally find a way out."

Then Mrs Carter seemed to think of something. She turned to the Jollyface twins and gave them the black skirt back.

"Take that along to your Mother," she said. "She bought it, and she's welcome to keep it. I'll send Teddy along with a jar of my tomato chutney as soon as I get home, I know she's partial to that!"

"And now, Ameliaranne," Mrs Carter
continued, "I want you to choose a little present
for yourself. Anything that you fancy you shall
have!"

"Oh!" gasped Ameliaranne, in surprise and
delight.

She thought for a moment, and then she
looked round for Miss Loveday. She went over
and whispered in her ear, and Miss Loveday
nodded and smiled at her.

Then Ameliaranne came back to Mrs Carter and said,

"Oh, please, I would love that pair of rabbity slippers for Wee William, but I am afraid they cost a lot of money."

"You shall have them whatever they cost," declared Mrs Carter promptly.

So she went up to Miss Loveday's stall, and
Ameliaranne watched anxiously as she looked
at the ticket that said 10p.

"Why, Ameliaranne, that's not dear!" she
cried. "And you've saved me all that money!"
The next minute Ameliaranne had the blue
rabbity slippers in her hand.

"Look!" she cried, showing them round to
everyone. "Aren't they lovely, and won't they
just suit our Wee William?"

And one and all agreed that they would.

PRINTED IN BELGIUM